DANCING DOGS

Charlotte and Emilio at the CIRCUS
by Barbara Westman

A Laura Geringer Book
An Imprint of HarperCollinsPublishers

For Arthur, Charlotte, and Emilio.
And for Mari, the elephant in
the Honolulu Zoo.

Dancing Dogs: Charlotte and Emilio at the Circus
Copyright © 1991 by Barbara Westman
Printed in the U.S.A. All rights reserved.
1 2 3 4 5 6 7 8 9 10
First Edition

Library of Congress Cataloging-in-Publication Data

Westman, Barbara.
Dancing dogs : Charlotte and Emilio at the circus / by Barbara
Westman.
p. cm.,
"A Laura Geringer book."
Summary: Stagestruck dogs Charlotte and Emilio become dancing
stars in their uncle's traveling circus.
ISBN 0-06-022459-2. — ISBN 0-06-022460-6 (lib. bdg.)
{1. Dogs—Fiction. 2. Circus—Fiction. 3. Dancing—Fiction.}
I. Title.
PZ7.W52625Dan 1991   90-23070
{E}—dc20   CIP
                                                                AC

St. Louis de Montfort Catholic School
Fishers, IN

Charlotte and Emilio's favorite uncle is bringing his circus to town.
The dogs gather around the poster in the town square.

Charlotte and Emilio haven't seen Uncle
Aubrey for a whole year. Emilio does a
cartwheel when the train arrives, and
Charlotte rushes forward with her
present—a big chocolate cake.
First to get off the train is their friend
Ruby the elephant.

While the tent goes up, Uncle Aubrey enjoys a picnic lunch with his family. Emilio is too excited to eat. Charlotte asks Uncle Aubrey if she and Emilio can be in the circus this year.

"No. You're not old enough yet," he answers, "but you can help the other animals get dressed if you like."

Charlotte and Emilio decide they want to
surprise Uncle Aubrey.
They ask the twins, Dotty and Dolly, to
teach them to dance some fancy steps.

Charlotte and Emilio practice and practice. Charlotte loves to dance. At first Emilio trips over his feet. But as soon as he puts on his costume, he does a lot better.

Charlotte and Emilio help Ruby get ready for the show. Ruby gets water all over the floor, and Emilio slips on the soap.

Backstage there is a lot of noise.
"We want to be in the circus too," Charlotte
tells Ruby. "We are very good dancers. Just
ask Dotty and Dolly."
Emilio doesn't hear Ruby's answer. He is
playing with the poodles' powder and
making a mess.

QUIET
PLEASE

The dogs line up to buy tickets from Ben the bulldog, but Charlotte and Emilio walk right in with Uncle Aubrey.

The Band strikes up "The Dog Town Mambo" and the circus is about to begin. "Take your seats, take your seats," cries Uncle Aubrey as the drums roll. "I am proud to present that daring duo, Dotty and Dolly, in their gravity-defying duet on the high wire." Emilio is having trouble with his cotton candy.

Tumblers and clowns come next.
Emilio can't sit still.

All the animals clap and stamp their feet as Tulip and True Blue skate around the ring. "Get ready—it's *time*," Charlotte warns Emilio. Emilio steps on a lady's foot as he and Charlotte make a quick exit.

The horses take their bows. Uncle Aubrey calls out, "And now the star of our show— Ruby the elephant—will dance the rumba. "But what's THIS?" he gasps. For there, directly in the spotlight, gracefully dancing the cha-cha, are Charlotte and Emilio!

And now they dance everybody's favorite—"The Dog Town Mambo." And they dance and dance and dance.

Uncle Aubrey gives Charlotte and Emilio a big hug. "I am proud of you," he says. "From now on you may be in my circus every year, Charlotte and Emilio—THE DANCING DOGS!"